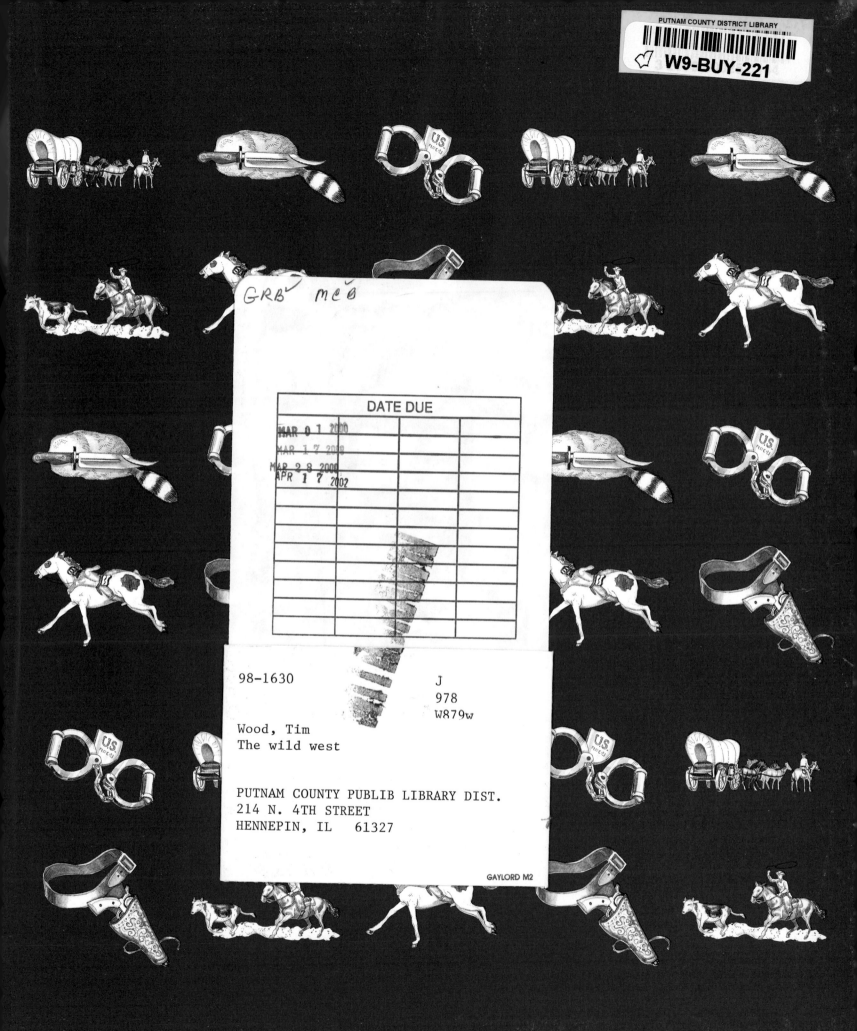

THE WILD
WEST

TIM WOOD

VIKING

Acknowledgments

The publishers would like to thank the following for permission to reproduce photographs in the book:

All photos from **Peter Newark's Western Americana** except page 13 top: **The Bridgeman Art Library/
Royal Ontario Museum, Toronto;** 15, 38: **Range/Bettmann**; 27: **The Bridgeman Art Library/
H.M. Tower of London Armouries**; 34: **Buffalo Bill Historical Center, Cody, NY/Vincent Mercaldo Collection.**

Illustrators
Peter Bull: maps, icons.
James Field: cover, 12–13, 26–27.
James G. Robbins: 16–17, 24–25, 32–33, 40–41.
Mark Stacey: 6–7, 14–15, 28–29, 38, 42, 44.
Steve Walsh: 20–21, 22–23, 30–31, 36–37.
Simon Williams: 8–9, 10–11, 18–19.

VIKING
Published by the Penguin Group
Penguin Putnam Inc., 375 Hudson Street, New York, New York 10014, U.S.A.
Penguin Books Ltd, 27 Wrights Lane, London W8 5TZ, England
Penguin Books Australia Ltd, Ringwood, Victoria, Australia
Penguin Books Canada Ltd, 10 Alcorn Avenue, Toronto, Ontario, Canada M4V 3B2
Penguin Books (N.Z.) Ltd, 182-190 Wairau Road, Auckland 10, New Zealand

Penguin Books Ltd, Registered Offices: Harmondsworth, Middlesex, England

First published in Great Britain by Heinemann Children's Reference,
a division of Reed Educational and Professional Publishing Ltd., 1996
Halley Court, Jordan Hill, Oxford OX2 8EJ

First published in the United States by Viking, a member of Penguin Putnam Inc., 1998

1 3 5 7 9 10 8 6 4 2

Copyright © Reed Educational and Professional Publishing Ltd., 1996

All rights reserved

Library of Congress Catalog Card Number: 97-60690

ISBN 0-670-87528-7

Printed and bound by Proost, Belgium.
See through pages printed by SMIC, France.

CONTENTS

THE WILD WEST

T he term "Wild West" refers to America's western frontier between about **1780** and the **1890s**. It was during this time, as people moved steadily over the Great Plains and the Rocky Mountains toward the Pacific Ocean, that the West was settled and the modern United States was born. The birth was not an easy or quiet event. It was dramatic, exciting, and sometimes violent.

EARLY SETTLEMENT

By the 17th century, several countries had claimed land in North America. Britain governed 13 colonies in the east. France held land near the St. Lawrence River and had founded Quebec, while explorers Marquette, Joliette, and La Salle explored the Mississippi and claimed land on both sides of the river, calling it Louisiana after King Louis XIV. The Dutch founded New Amsterdam (later renamed New York) in 1623. Spain expanded from the Caribbean into Florida, and from Central America into Mexico.

FRANCE, SPAIN, AND BRITAIN

During the 18th century, Britain, France, and Spain each attempted to dominate North America. Britain gained the advantage when, in 1763, the Peace of Paris granted Canada, parts of Florida, and most French lands east of the Mississippi to the British.

After 1865, wagon trains rolled almost continuously westward along the Santa Fe and Oregon Trails. This painting by Charles Russell (1864–1926) shows the boss of a wagon train. Russell worked as a trapper and cowboy. His paintings of the West often depict scenes of life on the trails.

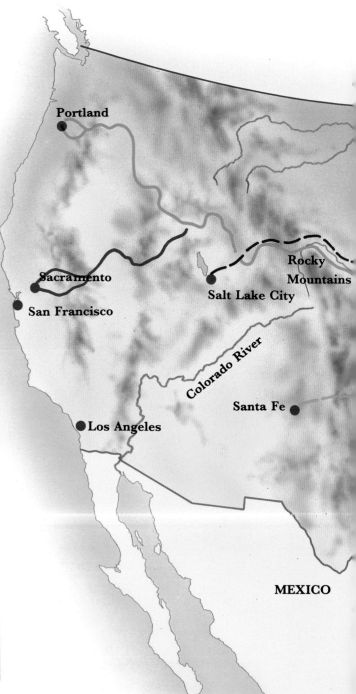

4

THE MOVING FRONTIER

In 1775, however, the colonies demanded independence from Britain, and the Revolutionary War began. By the time the war ended in 1783, the colonies had won their freedom. The western frontier of the United States was formed by the Appalachian Mountains. During the next hundred years U.S. territory expanded westward through a combination of exploration, wars, and land deals. By 1820, the frontier had reached the Mississippi River. The discovery of gold, and the desire for new land led to a great increase in westward emigration. These pioneers pushed the frontier into the "Wild West," across the Great Plains toward California.

THE WILD WEST ADVENTURE

Stories of the Wild West live on in the adventures of colorful characters such as Davy Crockett, Sitting Bull, Calamity Jane, Jesse James, and Wyatt Earp. Over the years, however, many of those stories have been exaggerated or dramatized beyond recognition. But frontier life really was dramatic. The West was a vast and untamed wilderness where pioneers faced the dangers of weather, hostile terrain, wild animals, and disease. There were cattle drives, stagecoaches, Indian wars, and gunfighters. The Wild West contained more than enough true adventure and real romance to thrill and inspire us today.

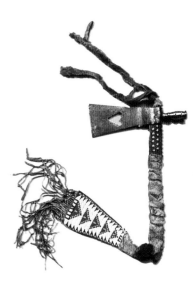

Native Americans, wrongly called Indians by Europeans who thought they had landed in the East Indies, created many beautiful artifacts. This pipe in the shape of a tomahawk was made by the Blackfoot tribe. They believed that the smoke from the pipe carried messages to the spirit world.

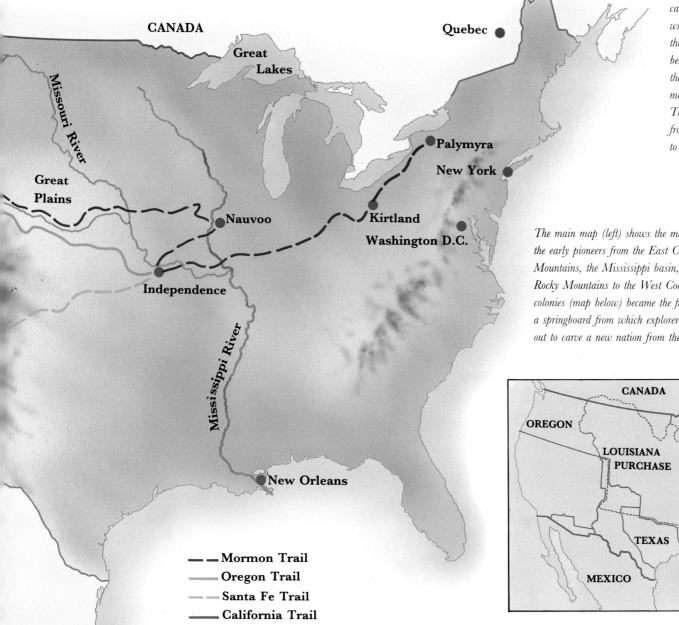

CANADA

Quebec

Great Lakes

Missouri River

Great Plains

Palymyra

New York

Nauvoo

Kirtland

Washington D.C.

Independence

Mississippi River

New Orleans

- ▬ ▬ Mormon Trail
- ▬▬ Oregon Trail
- ▬ ▬ Santa Fe Trail
- ▬▬ California Trail

The main map (left) shows the major trails, or routes, taken by the early pioneers from the East Coast across the Appalachian Mountains, the Mississippi basin, the Great Plains, and the Rocky Mountains to the West Coast. In 1783, the 13 original colonies (map below) became the first 13 states. The states were a springboard from which explorers, adventurers, and settlers set out to carve a new nation from the unsettled lands in the West.

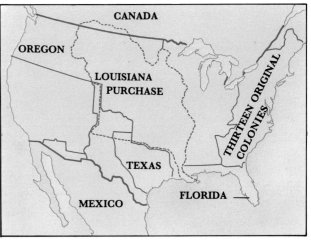

CANADA

OREGON

LOUISIANA PURCHASE

THIRTEEN ORIGINAL COLONIES

TEXAS

MEXICO

FLORIDA

FRONTIERSMEN

The first European settlers in the New World lived in tiny communities on the East Coast. As other settlers arrived, they either moved into established communities or looked for new lands. Little by little, the frontier began to move westward.

TENSION MOUNTS

By 1753, one million Americans lived in colonies along the eastern seaboard. Relations between the American colonists and Britain worsened steadily. The colonists resented paying taxes to Britain without having any say in their own government. "No taxation without representation" became the American rallying cry.

THE REVOLUTIONARY WAR

By 1765, a series of taxes called "Acts" (such as the Sugar Act) were levied on the American colonists by Britain. Outraged, the colonists began to rebel, and by 1775, war broke out. The Declaration of Independence was drafted and signed a year later. The last major battle was fought in 1781, when colonial armies defeated the British in Yorktown. In 1783, the Revolutionary War ended and the United States of America was born.

THE FIRST TRAILS

At that time the interior of the continent was a vast, unknown wilderness. Only small parts of the land had been explored by Europeans and very little had been mapped. The first trails into the interior were scouted by fur trappers.

Traders swapped beads, blankets, axes, and knives with local Indians for beaver, mink, fox, and otter furs. Some traders offered guns and alcohol. Few Native Americans were interested in trapping, so fur trading companies began to hire white colonists and Europeans as trappers. The fur trappers, also known as mountain men, held annual gatherings, called rendezvous, where they sold their furs and bought supplies for the following year. By 1800, the fur supply on the East Coast was nearly exhausted. But as trappers moved farther inland in search of animal furs, they pushed the frontier with them.

[The mountain man] always rode ahead, his body bent over his saddle-horn across which rested a long heavy rifle, his keen gray eyes peering from under the slouched brim of a flexible felt hat, black and shining with grease.

— George Ruxton —

Fur trappers learned many skills from the Native Americans. One of the most useful was how to build canoes. The canoe shown on the right had a wooden frame which was covered with bark cut from birch trees. The frontier had no proper trails, so water often offered the easiest routes for trappers and explorers. Birch-bark canoes were easy to paddle and light enough to portage (carry) between lakes and rivers. Furs were used to make gloves, muffs, wraps, and hats for fashionable people. But over-trapping and settlement of wild areas hurt the fur trade. The value of beaver skins fell sharply in 1830 when hatters began to use silk instead of fur.

ROUTES WESTWARD

In 1803, former army officers Meriwether Lewis and William Clark led a survey of the lands west of the Mississippi River. In 1805, Zebulon Pike explored the Great Plains. Some mountain men and trappers served as trailblazers, leading settlers through the unknown territories. Among them were William Becknell, who first traveled the Santa Fe Trail, Jedediah Smith, who explored the South Pass along the Oregon Trail, and Kit Carson, a scout who later helped to map the Oregon Trail. The Oregon Trail would become the most popular route west, carrying thousands of settlers to the Pacific Coast between the 1840s and 1850s.

MANIFEST DESTINY

Eager to lay claim to more territory, the government promoted the idea of "manifest destiny," which held that God had destined the United States to control all of North America. Rallying to the cry of "Westward, ho!" and eager to find better lives, settlers willingly complied.

Trappers set spring-loaded traps for small animals, and killed large animals, such as bears, with guns. Trappers moved around constantly resetting their traps.

Daniel Boone was one of the most famous mountain men. Mountain men went where no settlers had gone before. Each trip opened up another part of the wilderness.

Fur trappers resting on the trail. Trappers spent much of their time alone in the mountains. They only returned to civilization to sell their furs. When they met on the trail they loved to swap tall stories.

Whatever the immigrants did not take to their new homes, they had to make. They made sturdy furniture from logs split into slabs called puncheons. They carved smaller items, such as bowls and spoons. Women spun and wove all the cloth used to make clothes. Iron pots, tools, and china were treasured by the pioneers because they could not make these things themselves.

The purchase of the Louisiana Territory from France in 1803 doubled the size of the U.S. At the same time, industry was booming. America looked to thousands of hopeful immigrants to fill factory jobs as well as to help build the canals and railroads that would connect the country.

WHY THEY CAME

Most immigrants came to the U.S. to find a better life. The Irish came to escape poverty and famine. The Germans came to escape political unrest. Others came to escape religious and political persecution, overcrowded cities, and unemployment. They saw America as a land of opportunity where they could start a new life, and perhaps even make a fortune. Many newcomers were very poor, but they brought skills which became part of the American way of life.

WHERE THEY WENT

Before 1882, there were no restrictions on immigration to the U.S. Anyone could come and start a new life in America. Most immigrants arrived by ship. Many settled in eastern cities like Boston, New York, or Philadelphia, and went to work in the factories. Others moved west into Wisconsin, Iowa, and Missouri to farm, or joined the wagon trains traveling even farther West.

PIONEER FAMILIES

Most pioneer families traveled light, carrying only the barest essentials, such as food, tools, and weapons. Others took as much as they could carry on pack animals or in wagons. What they did not take with them into the wilderness, they would have to make themselves. Iron tools, seed, and household goods were highly prized.

FOOD AND CLOTHING

The pioneers ate mainly corn and meat. They ground corn into flour to make bread, cakes, and biscuits. They raised the cows, sheep, pigs, and chickens they had brought with them, and hunted for animals such as duck, turkey, wild pigs, and rabbits in the surrounding woods. They salted, dried, or smoked meat to preserve it. They grew vegetables, such as squash, beans, potatoes, turnips, and cabbages, and herbs including sage and dill in their gardens. Water and milk were the main drinks, with corn whiskey on special occasions. Honey and maple syrup were used to sweeten food.

Pioneers made their clothing from animal skins such as deerskin, or wove cloth from flax, cotton, or wool, or "linsey-woolsey"—a mixture of linen and wool. Men wore loose shirts and trousers with fur hats in winter and woven straw hats in summer. Women wore long dresses and aprons. In summer they wore bonnets to shield their skin from the sun. Children wore clothes similar to those worn by their parents, and often went barefoot or in moccasins.

Immigrants in the 1870s sighting the "Promised Land." The poorest immigrants, like the ones shown here, traveled in the cheapest "steerage" section of the ship.

Pioneers moved on to land that had never been farmed. The family lived in a simple shelter until the land was cleared, plowed, and planted with seed. Once the crops were growing, they built log cabins. Settlers on the Great Plains, where there were no trees, built sod houses out of thick mats of turf cut from the ground.

9

After 1830, more and more settlers moved west across the Mississippi. Most of them were aiming for California or the Oregon Territory and wanted to cross the Great Plains and the mountain ranges as quickly as they could. At this time, few settled on the plains. As they moved, the pioneers pushed the frontier west with them.

TEXAS

Expansion often brought conflict. In 1823 Stephen F. Austin had established an American colony in what was then Spanish Texas. The settlers farmed the land and ranched cattle; however, they disliked being controlled by the Mexican government. Relations between the Mexican government and Texas settlers deteriorated, and by 1835 the settlers began to demand liberty. The Mexican leader, Antonio de Santa Anna, was determined to crush the American revolt.

The two forces met head on at the Alamo, an old mission in the town of San Antonio.

THE ALAMO

The heroic defense of the Alamo became an important symbol for Texas and for the young nation. On February 23, 1836, 187 Texans, led by William Travis, along with Jim Bowie and Davy Crockett, prepared to hold off a Mexican army of over 5,000. The battle raged for 11 days. When Santa Anna's forces assaulted the crumbling walls, the Texans fought using their guns as clubs, with knives and bare hands. They were all killed. Their deaths gave Texans a new battle cry—"Remember the Alamo!" The battle gave General Sam Houston enough time to gather an army to defeat Santa Anna, after which Mexico was forced to grant Texas its independence.

THE MORMONS

Religious groups showed heroism of another kind, particularly the Mormons, or Latter-day Saints, who also played a leading role in opening up the West. In 1846, members of the Church of Jesus Christ of Latter-day Saints, a Christian sect, left Illinois and followed their leader, Brigham Young, westward across the Great Plains to find a Promised Land. They settled near the Great Salt Lake in Utah. The heat and dryness made the land hard to farm, but during the next 30 years the Mormons made the land bloom and built nearly 100 other settlements. Salt Lake City became a good stopping place for other travelers crossing the country.

Steam-powered paddleboats were an ideal form of transportation on the shallow Mississippi and Missouri rivers. Some were like floating palaces with luxurious cabins and gambling halls. River pilots could read the position of every bend, island, shallow, and sandbank on the rivers, even in the dark.

OREGON TERRITORY

In 1841, the first large wagon train set out on the Oregon Trail, carrying settlers lured by stories of the rich, green valleys of the Oregon Territory. The settlement that followed forced the U.S. and Britain to resolve a long-standing quarrel over the area. The result was the Oregon Treaty, which divided the territory along the 49th parallel. This line became the border between the U.S. and Canada.

Colonel William Travis, the Texan officer in command of the Alamo, announced "I shall never surrender or retreat." None of the Texan soldiers escaped from the mission. The only survivors were the wife of one of the Texan officers, her baby, her Mexican nurse, and a young boy.

QUARRELS WITH MEXICO

From 1846–1848, the U.S. and Mexico were at war. The peace treaty awarded the U.S. more than 390,000 square miles of land, including present-day California, Nevada, and Utah, as well as parts of Colorado, and Wyoming. In 1853, by the Gadsden Purchase, the U.S. bought the land that is now in southern Arizona and New Mexico. The route west had opened.

Mormons moving west. The Mormon church was founded in 1830 by Joseph Smith and grew rapidly. The Mormons moved to the remote Salt Lake area of Utah to escape the hostility and persecution they suffered in Missouri and Illinois. Utah became a state in 1896.

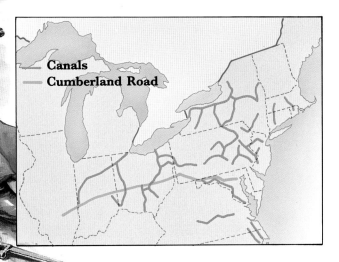

Settlers established a network of canals and roads for transportation of goods on the East Coast. The Cumberland Road, or National Highway, was the main route. But uniting the continent into one country was not yet a realistic goal. By the 1840s, however, the government had come to believe that the United States should control all the land in North America. This was called "Manifest Destiny" and became the goal of government policy.

Canals
Cumberland Road

NATIVE AMERICANS

An Apache ambush painted by Frederic Remington. The Apache lived in parts of Arizona, New Mexico, and Mexico. They were feared by other tribes and white settlers alike, partly because of their reputation as fierce warriors. The Apache were among the last of the Native Americans to be forced into submission by the government.

We started the story of the settlement of the Wild West in about 1783, when the U.S. won its war for independence. However, North America had already been inhabited for thousands of years. The first North Americans probably came from Asia about 50,000 years ago by walking across a land-bridge which, at that time, connected Siberia to Alaska.

NATIVE AMERICANS

There were about two million Native Americans in 1800. They were grouped in hundreds of tribes widely scattered throughout the continent. As a result they spoke different languages and had different lifestyles. Some farmed, and others hunted and fished. Some groups survived by doing all of these.

FARMERS AND HUNTERS

In different parts of the continent, Native Americans grew corn (that is, maize, which was later called "Indian corn"), potatoes, cassava, and sweet potatoes, in addition to many other types of food. They raised turkeys and hunted many species of wild animals, the most important of which was the buffalo. They grew tobacco, rubber plants, cotton, and many medicinal plants. Tribes that lived near the sea caught fish with nets, harpoons, spears, traps, and even bows and arrows. The lifestyle of each tribe greatly influenced the types of homes they built. More settled tribes, generally those who lived mainly by farming, built larger, more permanent homes out of wood or mud bricks. Nomadic hunting tribes, which followed herds of wild animals, such as buffalo, built portable homes such as tepees (tents).

EARLY FRIENDSHIP

The Native Americans were not very worried by the first settlers. To them the land was huge and there seemed to be enough room for all. The tribes traded for metal goods, horses, and, eventually, guns. But when settlers began to arrive in increasingly large numbers, the two groups came into conflict more frequently. Quarrels began as early as 1618, when the Jamestown colonists fought with local tribes. Hundreds were killed on both sides. Over the next 150 years the Iroquois, Shawnee, Ottawa, Chippewa, Creek, Cherokee, and Seminole peoples were driven out of their traditional hunting grounds east of the Mississippi and their lands turned into farms by settlers.

Forts were centers of trade with Native Americans. Fort Union on the Santa Fe Trail and Fort Laramie on the Oregon Trail each had large trading posts.

THE PLAINS INDIANS

Growing numbers of settlers from the East pushed the native tribes ever farther westward. Among the later native tribes to be affected by the pioneers were those who lived on the Great Plains. They were wanderers who followed the gigantic herds of buffalo that roamed freely over the land. Among them were the Sioux and the Cheyenne. Most white settlers thought of them as savages. They were to prove strong and determined opponents who fought to bring westward expansion to a halt.

This painting of a Native American encampment on Lake Huron was done in 1830 by Paul Kane. Kane shows the tepees, which were homes for many different tribes of Plains Indians. The tepees were made of buffalo skins stretched over frameworks made from branches. The buffalo skins had to be scraped clean, stretched out to dry in the sun, and then beaten to make them soft.

How Buffalo Were Used

A male buffalo could weigh nearly one ton. Each animal was an important source of meat.

Buffalo meat was dried to preserve it. The dried meat was called jerky.

Buffalo meat was also pounded with berries to make pemmican.

The shaggier parts of the skin were made into robes and ceremonial headdresses. Bones and horns were carved to make tools and other useful objects.

People used fat to protect their faces from the dry prairie winds and to make leather more supple.

Cured buffalo hide was used to make clothing, bedding, bags, moccasins, and tepees. It took 15–30 hides to make one tepee.

Uncured hide, called rawhide, was cut into strips and used as cord or rope. Small sections of hide were stretched over wooden frames to make drums.

13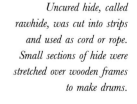

GOLD!

On January 24, 1848, James Marshall was building a sawmill in the Sacramento Valley when he spotted something glittering on the ground. In great excitement, he and his employer, John Sutter, tested the metal. It was gold!

GOLD FEVER
The news spread like wildfire. People everywhere became infected with "Gold Fever" and left their homes and jobs to set out for California. They came by two main routes. The sea trip around Cape Horn to San Francisco involved much discomfort in overcrowded ships. Often, when the ships arrived in San Francisco harbor, the crews deserted to join the Gold Rush and left the vessels in the harbor. The overland route from frontier settlements along the Mississippi and Missouri rivers and across the Great Plains was even more uncomfortable and dangerous.

At first the route over the rolling plains seemed easy. But gradually the sun, the dust, the endless expanse became wearing. The travelers faced the dangers of floods and storms. There were no trees, no firewood, and no grass, just mile after mile of choking dust. Many people and animals died of thirst.

I shall never forget that morning . . . [my] eye caught a glimpse of something shining at the bottom of the ditch. . . . It made my heart thump for I felt certain it was gold.

— *James Marshall* —

A gold prospector on his way to the diggings. Prospectors were called "Forty-niners" because the Gold Rush took place in 1849. Although prospectors helped to open up the West, most of them actually traveled eastward, starting in San Francisco and traveling inland to the Sierra Nevada mountains.

THE RACE TO THE MOUNTAINS

The journey became a race to reach the mountains before winter snows blocked the passes. The prospectors pushed and pulled their wagons up steep slopes and along rocky trails by brute force. Cholera claimed the lives of 5,000. Thousands more died of hunger, thirst, exhaustion, exposure, and lack of medical care. Yet still thousands more came. In 1848, there were 20,000 people in California. Just four years later, the population had increased tenfold.

The first arrivals staked their claims, and set up their tents or shacks. Shantytowns sprang up overnight. Some gold-rush towns, including Virginia City and Denver, survived after the Gold Rush. Others, such as Volcano, where $90,000,000 worth of gold was taken, became ghost towns when the gold ran out and the "Forty-niners" moved on.

A gold miner photographed in 1860. Thousands of people caught "gold fever," deserting their jobs, wives, and families to become prospectors. Notices reading "Gone to the Diggings" were common in shop windows in San Francisco. One estimate claimed that nearly three-quarters of all Californian men left home to seek gold; in all, some 80,000 people traveled to the gold fields.

A poster advertising a passage on the fast sailing ship Ocean Express *from New York's East River via Cape Horn to San Francisco in California. This was the method by which thousands of Easterners moved to the West Coast during the Gold Rush. Many of the prospectors who failed to make their fortunes stayed on anyway to start new lives in the West.*

Although it was called mining, most forms of prospecting involved washing vast amounts of sand to find tiny nuggets or grains of gold that sank to the bottom of the container. The miners shown here have built a sluice with slats across the base to catch the heavy grains.

PANNING FOR GOLD

The first prospectors to arrive in the area of a strike were placer miners. Placers were deposits of earth containing gold. One of the simplest methods of extracting this gold was panning. The prospector scooped topsoil into a metal pan. Swirling water around the pan carried off the dirt, leaving the heavier gold behind.

However, once the surface gold started to dwindle, the prospectors turned to more elaborate methods. One way was the sluice box, a U-shaped trough with a gentle slope. Slats fixed across the bottom of the trough (called riffles) caught the heavier particles of gold while the flow of water washed away the soil. Another way involved using hoses to wash away soil and gravel from areas that might hold gold deposits.

15

GOLD MINE

Prospectors were always in danger from bandits, as shown in the see-through scene. Mining settlements began as tent towns but soon more permanent wooden buildings were added, also shown in the see-through scene. Some inhabitants lived by stealing gold from miners or by "jumping their claims" (taking over their gold workings by force).

By the late **1850s,** panners and other prospectors had all but exhausted the surface gold deposits. Large mining companies moved in and took over.

THE END OF THE BOOM

A prospector's life was hard, and few became rich. Gold-rush towns could be dangerous places. Poor diet led to illnesses such as scurvy. Gold-rush towns also attracted criminals, gamblers, and saloon owners all determined to take their share of the miners' hard-earned wealth.

Drinking and gambling were the main recreations, and gunfights were common. There were few laws, and fewer law officials, so justice was usually carried out by the people.

Thieves and claim jumpers were often

1 **Prospectors**
2 **Bandits**
3 **Six-shot pistol**
4 **Shotgun**

hanged. In 1849, for instance, five bandits were sentenced to 39 lashes each for attempting to rob a Mexican gambler. Three of them were then accused of a murder and hanged by a drunken mob. For years after this, the town was called Hangtown.

When the boom ended, many prospectors went home. Some wandered off to new gold or silver strikes. The rest stayed on, either finding employment in a mining company or turning to work such as farming or shopkeeping.

The Gold Rush did attract fortune hunters, but it also brought traders, salesmen, and farmers to the West. New villages, towns, roads, and railroads were built. The Gold Rush brought new settlers and new wealth, which, in turn, helped to stimulate industrial growth.

If the gold strike was large enough, more prospectors poured into the town. More buildings sprang up and some of the first to be finished were saloons. The prospectors worked hard, but soon spent everything they earned just keeping alive because the prices of food and tools in gold-rush towns soared to amazingly high levels. Once the gold deposits that were near the surface had been found, mining became harder work. At this stage, large mining companies moved in to exploit the deep deposits of gold. This needed expensive machinary to extract the metal from the ore, as shown in the see-through scene. When the gold ran out, the town would be abandoned, becoming a "ghost town."

1 **Unloading ore**
2 **Crushers and sludgers**
3 **Shakers to remove lead and silver**
4 **Extractors**
5 **Settling tanks to remove remaining impurities**
6 **Boiler**

WAGON TRAINS

After the Civil War ended in 1865, westward migration intensified. Settlers began to pour over the Great Plains. They often traveled in large groups for protection, joining wagon trains traveling along the Oregon, California, or Santa Fe Trails.

Most settlers traveled in simple wagons known as "Prairie Schooners," because the white canvas tops of the wagons looked like the sails of ships as they moved across the open prairies. Settlers stopped only to camp or to make repairs.

Those who crossed the plains . . . never forgot the . . . thirst, the intense heat and bitter cold, the craving hunger, and utter physical exhaustion of the trail.

— *Octavius T. Howe* —

WAGON TRAIN
Most wagon trains set out from frontier towns such as Independence, Missouri, starting their journey as soon as the warm spring weather arrived. A good-sized wagon train contained about 100 families, although there were some much larger ones. Those traveling all the way across the country would stay with the wagon train for nearly six months. Other travelers joined and left at different places, depending on their starting points and destinations. Although they were strangers at the beginning of the journey, the families on the wagon train had to learn to trust and help each other.

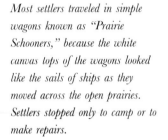

WAGONS

The covered wagon was the best form of transportation for a whole family and all its possessions. The most popular wagon was the Conestoga. It had a boat-shaped body, which was often painted blue, with red wheels. The wagon curved up at the front and rear to keep its contents from falling out on steep slopes. The body was covered with a white canvas top supported by iron hoops. Each wagon train elected a leader and hired a scout to guide them. Some scouts, such as Jim Bridger and Kit Carson, became very famous. Some of the trails were so heavily traveled that even today, deep wheel ruts can still be found in undeveloped areas of the West.

DANGERS OF THE TRAIL

In Western films, wagon trains are often shown being attacked by Native Americans. In fact before 1855, most Native Americans were friendly to wagon trains, helping them along the trail, hunting for them, and trading with them. However, some deadly attacks did occur. As more and more families crossed the Great Plains and began to settle on tribal lands, the Native Americans' way of life and the herds of buffalo on which they depended were threatened. Some tribes became hostile, and attacks on wagon trains increased. Even so, there were more deaths from accidents and diseases—such as smallpox and cholera—than there were from Indian attacks.

Pioneers resting on the trail. The journey west was very exhausting. There were few chances for rest and relaxation except in the evening when people gathered around the campfire to tell stories and sing.

THE RACE

A wagon covered only about 15 miles a day, and had to stop often for repairs. Travelers sometimes stopped at army posts to trade for food or supplies. It was a race to cross the mountains before winter. In 1846, tragedy struck a wagon train, the Donner Party, when they became snowbound in a mountain pass. Half the people died during the terrible winter. Others lived by cannibalizing the bodies of those who had died.

At night, wagons formed a circle (right) that served as a kind of fort, and penned in the livestock.

19

HOMESTEADERS

In 1862, the Homestead Act granted 160 acres of land to any U.S. citizen who would live on it and farm it for five years. Much of the best land was being bought by railroad companies who resold it for big profits. By 1900, the act had provided farms and homes for 600,000 families in the West.

Settlers in a land rush raced to stake their claims.

Farmers on the Great Plains were often called "sod busters" because they broke up the hard sod with their plows. The shortage of wood forced them to use sod to make their houses. Sod houses were warm, but dusty and dirty inside. Pests, such as mice and snakes, made nests in hollows in the walls.

SETTLING DOWN

Within 20 years, settlers had populated Kansas, Nebraska, Dakota, Wyoming, and Montana. Oklahoma was the only remaining unsettled land. However, much of the land there was designated as part of the Indian Territory where native tribes were forced to relocate.

PUMPS AND BARBED WIRE

Prairie farmers had to learn new techniques to grow crops. They irrigated their land with water drawn from deep underground by small pumps. They

PROBLEMS

The new settlers built their homesteads on the Great Plains where farming was much more difficult than it was in the fertile valleys of the Oregon Territory. The vast open grassland was more suitable for ranching than for growing crops. Rainfall was low, and timber for building and fencing was scarce. Pioneer farmers faced terrible droughts, hot dry winds that raised choking dust storms, plagues of grasshoppers, prairie fires, violent hailstorms that flattened crops, tornadoes that could carry away entire houses and barns, and winter storms that dumped heavy snows on them.

Generosity between neighbors was an important part of frontier life. People would share crops, animals, tools, or money to help a neighbor in trouble.

protected their fields from wandering cattle with barbed wire, invented in 1874 by an Illinois farmer to keep dogs away from his wife's flowers.

FRONTIER LIFE

Frontier life was very hard work. The men did heavy work such as plowing and digging wells. Everyone helped with planting, weeding, and harvesting. Women performed many tasks including helping to farm the land, raising animals, teaching the children, and washing clothes. They spun thread, wove the thread into cloth, and made clothes. They also canned and preserved food and cooked meals. This grueling work, added to childbearing, sickness, and fear of attacks, made most pioneer women old before the age of 40.

BEING NEIGHBORLY

Their isolation and common hardships made most frontier settlers friendly and hospitable. They generally trusted other people. Doors were seldom locked and a man's word was as good as his bond. Many merchants sold items on credit, or lent money freely. They trusted their customers to pay their bills. But the isolation did create loneliness. The pioneer family's nearest neighbors could be a day's ride away. For months on end many people were visited only by a circuit rider (traveling preacher). Circuit riders helped bring a sense of peace and order to the frontier.

A pioneer cabin is shown above. Pioneers lived very simple lives with few comforts. A cast-iron stove was one of the most important household possessions because it provided heat as well as a means of cooking. Some homes, however, relied on fireplaces for cooking and heating.

The first pioneers had to take everything with them or make it themselves. After 1872, settlers could buy almost anything they wanted through mail-order catalogs. This page from a Sears & Roebuck catalog shows some of the farming machines that could be bought by mail order.

21

COWBOYS

The first cowboys were Texans who stole cattle from Mexican ranches. Later, the Texans learned how to ranch cattle of their own. During the Civil War many Texans went away to fight for the South. They returned to find their land ruined. There were huge herds of wild, ownerless cattle roaming the open range, but meat prices were low in Texas and they were worth almost nothing. Meat prices were ten times higher in growing northern cities. The Texans realized they could make fortunes if they could get the cattle in large numbers to the north.

NORTH TO THE RAILROAD

In 1866, Texas cowboys drove the first herds 1,500 miles northward to the nearest railhead in Missouri. Along the way, ranchers and farmers often attacked and scattered these herds. They feared Texas cattle had fever and would infect their own herds.

An Illinois businessman, Joseph G. McCoy, scouted a new place for cattlemen and buyers to meet. He built corrals (pens) and stockyards (markets) on the Kansas Pacific Railroad. Texas ranchers drove their cattle to this new depot along the Chisholm Trail. The new depot, called Abilene, soon became a booming town, and the Texas cattle industry was born.

THE ROUNDUP

Once the route north was established, cattle drives became regular events. For most of the year the cattle roamed freely on the range. In the spring, cowboys rounded up all the cattle they could find and herded them together. Then the drive crew started the herd, which could contain several thousand head of cattle, on the trail northward.

The first cattle were brought to America by the Spanish. Texas Longhorns are descendants of these animals. They are tough, sure-footed cattle with long legs and huge horns to fight off predators such as wolves and cougars.

THE CATTLE DRIVE

The drive crew was led by the trail boss, often the owner, who was in charge of up to a dozen cowboys. The crew was accompanied by a chuckwagon that was driven by the cook. Younger cowboys, called wranglers, watched over the spare horses and brought up the rear of the herd. A cattle drive could last up to six months. The crew drove the herd from one watering place to the next. They kept the herd in one group, rounding up strays and trying to keep a slow but steady pace. The cowboys faced many dangers including floods, sandstorms, snakebites, and attacks by Native Americans. But most cowboys probably died from illness or from injuries they received falling off their horses.

CATTLE TRAILS

In 1871, more than 700,000 cattle traveled the Chisholm Trail, which became the major route from San Antonio, Texas, to Abilene in Kansas. However, by the mid-1870s, the Chisholm Trail became less important as railheads and settlements moved farther west. By 1876, Dodge City had become the main depot. Cattle towns like Dodge City became famous as lawless towns populated by gamblers, gunmen, and rough cowboys who frequented brothels and saloons.

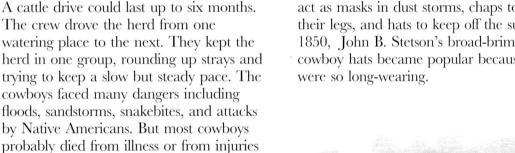

The chuckwagon was the mobile headquarters of a drive crew. In it were stored a large chuck box with drawers for food, pans, water barrel, toolbox, medicines, weapons, and bedrolls. Cooking was done on an open fire.

COWBOY CLOTHES

Most cowboys came from the South. Many wore bandanas to protect their necks and act as masks in dust storms, chaps to protect their legs, and hats to keep off the sun. After 1850, John B. Stetson's broad-brimmed cowboy hats became popular because they were so long-wearing.

Loading cattle at Abilene. Cowboys were sometimes called cowpokes because they poked the cattle onto the trucks with long sticks. Once the cattle were loaded, the cowboys were paid their wages. After a good meal and a bath, many were lured into spending their earnings in saloons and gambling halls.

CATTLE RANCH

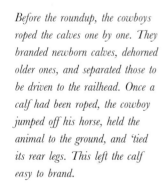

The picture shows a working cattle ranch. The inset pictures show cowboys rounding up, roping, and branding calves before a cattle drive.

The first ranchers did not own any land. Each simply built a shack on an area of open range, and lived in it. They rounded up any wild cattle that were wandering in the area and claimed them as their own by branding them. They guarded their herds against rustlers.

RANCH HOUSES

As ranching became more profitable and the trails northward more established, ranchers built more permanent homes. Many ranches in the south were made of adobe (mud bricks). Ranch houses farther north were generally built from wood. The bunkhouse was where the cowboys slept. The cookhouse was where they ate.

PROBLEMS OF RANCHING

The weather could be a major problem for ranchers. In many places the range was overcrowded and there was not enough grass for the cattle. In 1886, the winter temperature fell to 46 degrees below zero, and thousands of cattle froze to death. Drought followed through the next two summers and many large cattle ranches went bankrupt.

24

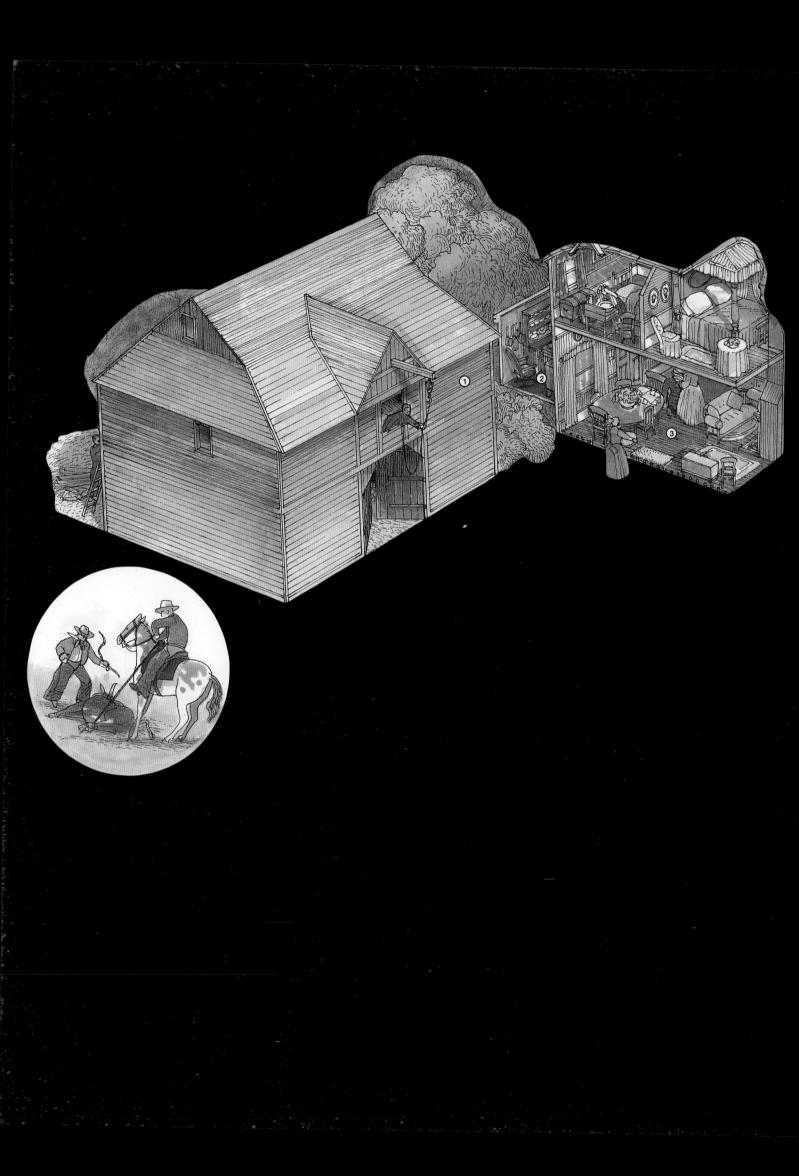

1	Barn	7	Cattle from range
2	Kitchen		
3	Living room	8	Mess room
4	Cookhouse	9	Bunkhouse
5	Bath house	10	Trail boss's bedroom
6	Chuckwagon		

Smart ranchers thought of ways to protect their cattle from drought and famine. They built pumps to draw water from underground and had extra feed sent in by rail to store in their barns.

BARBED WIRE

The use of barbed wire to enclose farmland became popular in the 1870s. However, most ranchers hated barbed wire because it allowed settlers to fence and farm sections of the open range that cattlemen wanted to see left open. The West became divided over the issue. Fence-cutting and even shootings were not uncommon.

SHEEP

After 1850, sheep appeared on the range. Sheep were raised for their wool and meat. Cattle ranchers hated them because they thought that sheep would ruin the land. In fact, sheep eat short grass and cattle eat long grass. Before it was known that grass that is grazed by sheep actually grows stronger and is better for cattle, range wars between sheep and cattle ranchers developed.

THE END OF THE COWBOY

By 1890 most of the range was fenced. The completion of the railroad ended the need for long cattle drives. The time of the cowboy was over. But stories and songs would keep the myth of the cowboy alive.

Some ranches were enormous. In 1880, the XIT ranch in Texas was nearly 5,000 square miles, and contained over 150,000 heads of cattle. Each ranch had its own brand to identify its cattle. Many brands showed the initials of the ranch owner, such as JA for John Adair, or simple pictures, such as hearts, squares, or rocking chairs. Rustlers often changed brands by re-branding the calves with "running irons" that disguised the original marks.

THE INDIAN WARS

The Native American tribes were not especially troubled by the first pioneers. The land was huge and there seemed to be enough room for all. But as time passed, the settlers poured west in ever increasing numbers, killing thousands of buffalo and taking over tribal hunting grounds to make farms and ranches.

THE TRAIL OF TEARS

The government set up reservations where tribes were to be relocated out of the way of advancing settlers. In the winter of 1838, over 15,000 Cherokees from northwestern Georgia and northeastern Alabama were forced to march across the Mississippi to a reservation in Oklahoma. Thousands died on the 1,200-mile journey, which became known as the "Trail of Tears."

At first, Indians stole cattle and raided isolated targets such as farms and wagon trains. Some settlers lived close to forts, but most had to protect their own homes when attacked.

RESERVATIONS

Reservations were usually far from tribal lands in some remote or barren area. In 1834, the government had created the Indian Territory in the Great Plains— primarily lands that today make up the state of Oklahoma. A peace treaty promised the tribes resettled there that they could remain "as long as the rivers shall run and the grass shall grow." But this was to be an empty promise. Soon more settlers arrived. The government did nothing to uphold the rights of the tribes, so the Indians fought back.

This painting by Charles Shreyvogel, called The Duel, *shows a cavalryman and an Indian warrior fighting hand to hand with saber and tomahawk. In fact, Native Americans were rarely on equal terms with the cavalry and stood little chance against the modern weapons, such as repeating rifles, machine guns, and cannons, used by the U.S. army.*

WAR AGAINST THE SIOUX

The government sent soldiers to restore order, and forts were built to keep the peace. In 1854, an army patrol was sent to a Sioux village to recover a lost cow. The chief, Conquering Bear, tried to resolve the matter peacefully, but shots were fired. The army officer and his 18 soldiers were killed. In the following year the army massacred 136 Sioux men, women, and children at the village of Ash Hollow in revenge. It was the first major incident in the Sioux wars, which lasted until 1890.

THE DISCOVERY OF GOLD

The wars began as a series of isolated raids and ambushes. Then in 1874, gold was discovered in the sacred Black Hills of the Dakota Territory. Control of Dakota had been granted to the Sioux in an 1868 treaty, but thousands of miners poured in anyhow. The Sioux chiefs realized that unless they fought to preserve their way of life, they would be swept away. The whole Sioux nation, with its allies the Cheyenne and the Arapaho, went on the warpath.

For 50 years the Apaches had resisted U.S. domination. This resistance came to an end in 1886 when the Apache chief, Geronimo, surrendered at Skeleton Canyon in Arizona.

ATROCITIES

Outnumbered, scattered, divided among themselves, and with few modern weapons, the Indians stood little chance against an army equipped with rifles and cannons. There were many examples of atrocities by both sides. In 1862, about 800 settlers were killed by Sioux warriors. But, generally, it was the tribes who suffered the most. For example, in 1864 soldiers attacked a Cheyenne camp at Sand Creek, Colorado, massacring over 200 men, women, and children. What the army called great victories, the Indians saw as the White Man's treachery.

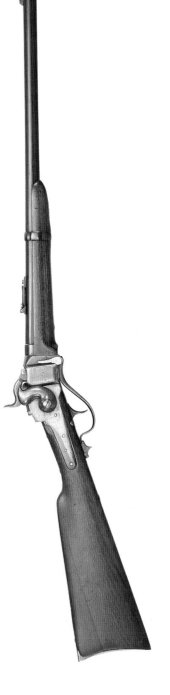

A Sharp's .50 caliber Buffalo rifle. As railroads moved west, the companies hired hunters to supply their workers with meat. One of the most famous was William F. "Buffalo Bill" Cody, who supplied buffalo meat for workers on the Kansas Pacific Railroad in 1867–68. He killed 4,280 buffalo in 18 months. Hunters, who virtually wiped out the buffalo, probably did more than any other people to destroy the traditional way of life of the Native Americans.

The government sent the army to the frontier to make it safe for settlers. Foot soldiers were too slow to fight mounted Indians and patrol the vast wilderness. This job went mainly to the U.S. cavalry.

THE ROLE OF THE ARMY

The army was based in forts built to protect the trails used by settlers moving west. Settlers and traders often lived close to the forts for protection. In remote areas, the army was often the only authority. Officers had to sort out disputes among local people. But the army's main role was controlling the Indians. The government hoped to keep the peace by making treaties. But these were often broken and some tribes resented being forced to live on reservations. As a result, the army became more aggressive. When gold was found in the Black Hills of the Dakota Territory in 1874, the Sioux refused to give up the hills. After treaty attempts failed, the army moved in to force them out.

A .44 caliber Colt army revolver. Variations of this six-shot pistol were used throughout the West. The Texas Rangers were the first force to use the weapon, invented by Samuel Colt in 1836.

A settler is greeted at a fort by its commander. Army forts generally had tall wooden stockades around them with towers and cannons for extra protection. Inside were barracks for the soldiers and stables for horses. At times the frontier moved so quickly that, when orders from Washington reached what had been the frontier, the settlers had moved on. The army was often building its forts many miles behind the rapidly advancing settlers.

There was no escape for the Indians. The army relentlessly pursued them into the remotest areas, using Indian scouts to help track down war parties. The army had better weapons than the Indians but did not win every skirmish. Both sides usually took no prisoners, killing any captives.

CRAZY HORSE AND SITTING BULL

In 1877, Crazy Horse was arrested and killed by his guards, who stabbed him with a bayonet. In 1890, Sitting Bull was shot dead for resisting arrest. Shortly after, the Seventh Cavalry had their revenge for Custer's death when they followed the Sioux chief Big Foot to his village on Wounded Knee Creek. The chief surrendered but the soldiers slaughtered every Sioux in the village, including women and children.

FAMOUS WESTERNERS

Many westerners served in the army. Buffalo Bill was Chief of Scouts for the Fifth Cavalry. Wild Bill Hickok, gambler and gunfighter, was a scout for Custer.

The Texas Rangers were formed in 1826. They guarded the frontiers, protected white settlers from Indians and Mexican bandits, and acted as peace officers. The Rangers were volunteers. They were all expert horsemen and were highly trained in the skills of marksmanship (shooting) and tracking.

BATTLE OF LITTLE BIGHORN

In June 1876, Arapahos, Cheyenne, and many Sioux tribes led by Sitting Bull and Crazy Horse were camped near the Little Bighorn river in Montana. The Seventh Cavalry led by General Custer was sent in to scout. After dividing his regiment, Custer attacked. All 250 men in his command were killed. According to legend Custer himself was the last to fall, although there is no evidence for this. Outraged at what was regarded as a terrible defeat, the American public demanded revenge for Custer's death. The army set about disposing of the remaining Sioux resistance.

These African-American soldiers of the Ninth Cavalry were nicknamed the "Buffalo Soldiers" by Native Americans. The best-known army unit fighting in the Indian Wars was the Seventh Cavalry. One of its most famous commanders was General George Armstrong Custer. Custer had earned a reputation for bravery during the Civil War, but many thought he was a glory hunter.

Before the arrival of cowboys, miners, and settlers, the West was a vast wilderness. Towns formed when groups of people settled in one place, usually to make money. Frontier towns grew quickly, so everything about them was rough.

This painting by C. M. Russell shows a gunfight over a card game in a frontier town. Frontier towns could be wild and lawless places. Cowboys, rewarding themselves with whiskey at the end of a long cattle drive, often became quarrelsome, and gunplay was sometimes the result.

[Abilene is] A very small dead place, consisting of about a dozen log huts—low small rude affairs, four-fifths of which were covered with dirt for roofing.

—*Joseph G. McCoy*

SHANTYTOWNS

Many new towns started as shanytowns, with tents and shacks hastily put up. The earliest towns lacked basic facilities such as public water and sewage systems. Buildings went up along the rutted dirt trail, which became the main street. Trading posts and general stores were the most important buildings. Some towns also had saloons, dance halls, or gambling parlors.

STORES AND OFFICES

Every town had a general store that sold hardware, dry goods such as cloth, tobacco, pots and pans, guns and ammunition, as well as mining tools, gunpowder, barbed wire, farming tools, or whatever else local people might need.

In a farming area, there would be a land office where people could register claims. In a mining area, there would be an assayer's office where miners could have their finds tested and valued. In a cow town, there might be a railroad station with stockyards and corrals. Where there was a railroad station, there would often be a telegraph office, because the wires ran alongside the railroad tracks. Most towns also had stables, a hotel, a blacksmith's shop, and a post office.

The general store was a center of town life. Storekeepers were often among the town leaders.

PEACEFUL TOWNS

With the appearance of order, new buildings sprang up. More homes were built on the outskirts of town. As local vigilance committees were replaced by law officers, a sheriff's office with a jail was needed. Churches and schools began to multiply. The church and schoolroom became the focal points of respectable life.

Guthrie, Oklahoma, in 1893. Although this was one of the last frontier towns, the photo shows how many boom towns grew. The first buildings were tents or shacks. Within a month Guthrie had a hotel, newspapers, stores, restaurants, and many saloons.

Mining camps, cow towns, and railroad towns all relied on stores to supply their needs. Storekeepers stocked goods such as tools, weapons, clothes, farm implements, and food.

The saloon was the chief form of entertainment for men. Most towns had one saloon or more for each 100 inhabitants. Many sold only whiskey made from pure alcohol.

Once a town became established, a school was built and a schoolteacher—usually female—was hired. Most schools were built from wood and had a single room where the children were taught.

CITIZENS

Growing towns attracted rowdy cowboys, gamblers, and gunslingers. But they also attracted more respectable people such as blacksmiths, merchants, teachers, ministers, and shopkeepers who wanted peace as well as prosperity in their town, and appointed law officers to restore law and order.

BRINGING PEACE

By 1885, even cities like Dodge City, the largest cattle market in the world and one of the rowdiest places in the West, were changing their ways. The local traders disliked the wild image of their community, which they feared was hurting cattle sales. They closed the saloons and got rid of lawless elements. A fire in 1885 burned down the last of the shanties and paved the way for a new, peaceful city.

31

A FRONTIER TOWN

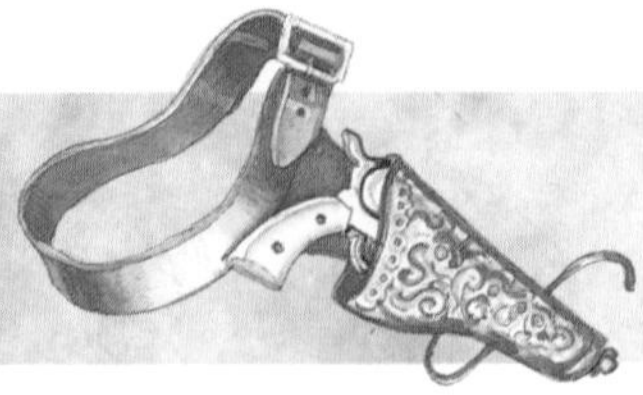

This illustration shows the daily life along the main street of a frontier town. The see-through scene shows a gunfight taking place in the street and the insides of the buildings.

Most buildings in frontier towns were made of wood, which was often the most plentiful and easily available building material. On the Great Plains, where there was a shortage of trees, timber and other building materials were brought in by wagon or by rail.

BUILDING DESIGN

Most buildings were box shapes with pitched roofs. Roofs made with wooden shingles were common. Most buildings had only a single story, but stores and hotels might have two or more. Many of the biggest buildings had false fronts and notice boards advertising what went on inside. As a town became permanent, some buildings were built in stone, and streets were paved.

SIDEWALKS AND RAILS

The streets in frontier towns were unpaved. In summer, passing travelers kicked up clouds of choking dust. When it rained, the streets became swamps. As time passed and a town became more established, the main streets might have raised wooden sidewalks that allowed pedestrians to walk down the side of the road without becoming dirty. In front of the wooden sidewalks were hitching posts where riders could tether their horses.

WIDE STREETS

Many western towns were deliberately laid out with wide streets: 98 feet or more was common. The main streets in Salt Lake City were even bigger, 131 feet wide with 23-foot-wide sidewalks. The streets were wide enough to allow a team of oxen pulling a wagon to turn in the road. Later, these wide streets proved ideal for building cable car systems. The use of cable cars then encouraged the growth of sprawling suburbs.

1	Outlaws
2	Lawmen
3	Bar
4	Hotel
5	Stables
6	Sheriff
7	Jail
8	General store
9	Stagecoach
10	Frightened horse

Outside the general store and the jail. A stagecoach waits for passengers, and a supply wagon is unloaded outside the store. The see-through scene shows the sheriff confronting gunmen trying to free a prisoner.

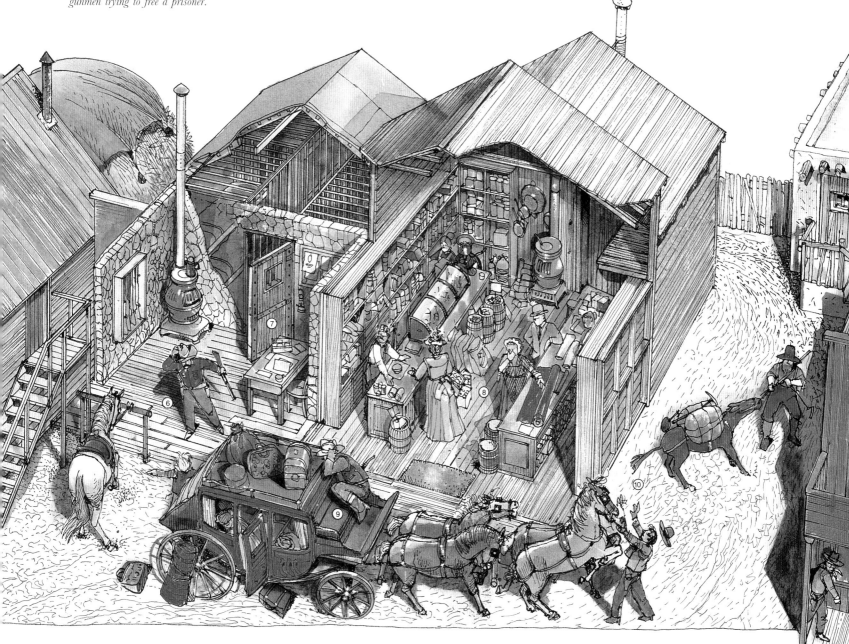

33

OUTLAWS

R emote settlements were easy targets for outlaws. Making and enforcing frontier laws had to be done by local people, usually by forming "vigilance committees" or vigilante groups to deal with criminals.

CRIME IN THE WEST

The West could be a violent place. Frontier people were tough, independent, and used to settling their own problems. Most people did not look for trouble, but if trouble came, they did not back down.

GUNSLINGERS

Brawls and gunfights were common, especially in boom towns such as Dodge City and Abilene, which became notorious for the rowdy, violent behavior of drunken cowboys, gamblers, and gunslingers. Arguments could easily end in murder. The smallest insult could result in a gunfight.

One of the most famous gunslingers was John Wesley Hardin, who boasted he had killed 44 men. One of them was a man in the next hotel room who annoyed Hardin by snoring! Although gunslingers or cowboys could make life uncomfortable or even dangerous in a town, it was the Civil War that created a new type of outlaw for whom robbery and murder was a way of life.

Dime novels dramatized the lives of many Western characters. As a result, it is difficult to know how much of Billy the Kid's "life story" is really true. The common belief that he killed 21 men—one for every year of his own life—is probably false. Experts think that he killed only about six.

Billy the Kid worked as a cowboy and rustler, and became involved in the Lincoln County Cattle War. He was killed by Sheriff Pat Garrett in 1881.

Belle Starr (1848–89) was in Quantrill's gang. She and her husband, Sam Starr, an Irish Cherokee, made their Oklahoma home into an outlaw retreat.

KANSAS–MISSOURI STRUGGLE

Some of the worst frontier violence took place in Kansas and Missouri. In 1854, Congress ruled that new states had to decide for themselves whether to be free states or slave states. The state of Kansas was the center of the anti-slavery movement, while neighboring Missouri was pro-slavery. When Missouri citizens started to vote in Kansas, quarrels between supporters and opponents of slavery led to killings, burnings, and lootings.

This quarrel became more intense during the Civil War. In 1863, a Confederate guerilla band known as Quantrill's Raiders, led by William Quantrill, attacked the town of Lawrence, Kansas, killing 150 men, women, and children. After the war Quantrill's Raiders were declared outlaws. Among them were Frank and Jesse James.

JESSE JAMES

From 1865 to 1882, the James Gang carried out the worst crime wave ever experienced in the West. Unlike other outlaws who had remote hideouts, the James Gang hid at Jesse's stepfather's farm in Clay County, Missouri. They commited the first bank robbery in the U.S. in 1866, and the first train robbery in 1872. They were copied by other outlaws, such as the Daltons and the Wild Bunch, who rampaged all over Colorado.

> ### I never in my life willingly hurt man, woman or child—unless they hurt me first. Then I made them pay.
>
> —— *Oliver M. Lee* ——

A group of cowboys running off cattle rustlers. For some men, stealing another person's cattle seemed an easy, if dangerous, way of making money.

NOTICE!
TO THIEVES, THUGS, FAKIRS
AND BUNKO-STEERERS,
Among Whom Are
J. J. HARLIN, alias "OFF WHEELER;" SAW DUST CHARLIE, WM. HEDGES, BILLY TEE KID, Billy Mullin, Little Jack, The Cuter, Pock-Marked Kid, and about Twenty Others:
If Found within the Limits of this City after TEN O'CLOCK P. M., this Night, you will be Invited to attend a GRAND NECK-TIE PARTY,
The Expense of which will be borne by
100 Substantial Citizens.
Las Vegas March 24th, 1882.

A vigilante notice of punishment to outlaws and criminals in 1882. Improved communications such as the telegraph and newspapers forced outlaws into increasingly remote areas. Eventually there was no place left to hide.

The Wild Bunch or "Hole in the Wall Gang" (after their remote Wyoming hideout): Kid Curry (back right); Butch Cassidy (front right); Sundance Kid (front left).

A bearded Jesse James (1847–1882) committed robberies in Missouri and Kansas. He was betrayed and shot in the back by cousin and "friend," Robert Ford.

THE LAWMEN

A s the frontier moved west, many communities were without a justice system. They had no law officers and relied instead on vigilantes to enforce the peace. Even after they became states, many areas still had no laws. In 1871, for example, the council in Ellsworth, Kansas, appointed a marshal. It was only then that they realized the marshal had no laws to enforce!

LAWS AND COURTS

Once states officially became part of the U.S., they introduced a legal system and courts with officially appointed judges. Trial by jury replaced hangings and vigilantes. Circuit judges who traveled from place to place to hold their courts brought the law to more remote areas. Some judges believed in giving the strongest punishments. One of the most notorious of these "hanging judges" was Judge Isaac C. Parker, who in 21 years sent 160 criminals to their deaths while his deputies shot dead another 65.

Judge Roy Bean (1825–1903) was one of the most colorful law officers. He owned a saloon in the railroad construction camp at Vinegaroon, Texas. He renamed the settlement Langtry (after Lillie Langtry, an actress he admired) and made himself justice of the peace. He held his court in the bar shown here.

LAWMEN

Some areas of the West were very violent. In Texas, Wyoming, and Arizona, gunslingers hired by rival cattle barons fought vicious range wars. The James Gang and the Younger Boys terrorized Kansas and Missouri. In some places, local people defended themselves. The Dalton Gang, for example, were gunned down by citizens during a disastrous attempt to rob two banks in Coffeyville, Kansas, at the same time! But most communities relied on law officers.

Lawmen were supposed to be elected but often the job went to the first brave man to volunteer. Sheriffs (in charge of counties) and marshals (in charge of towns) appointed deputies to help them and used local people to form posses when pursuing suspects. U.S. marshals and deputy marshals were the only law officers who could operate anywhere in the country.

Anyone can bring in a dead man, but to my way of thinking a good [law] officer is one that brings them in alive.

— *Tom Smith* —

DEDICATED LAWMEN

Most of the famous lawmen made their reputations taming cow towns such as Dodge and Abilene. Many lawmen were honest, dedicated upholders of the law. Two legendary lawmen were Bill Tilghman and Bat Masterson.

Tilghman, who was marshal of Dodge City in 1885 and U.S. deputy marshal in Oklahoma, never drew his gun except as a last resort. Bat Masterson was deputy sheriff of Dodge City in 1876, and later helped to bring law and order to the towns of Deadwood and Tombstone.

CORRUPT LAWMEN

Other officers took the job for the money or power it gave them. The grateful citizens of Caldwell so admired their marshal, Henry Brown, that they presented him with a rifle. A year later they hanged him for organizing a bank robbery!

Wild Bill Hickok, marshal of Abilene, was a crack shot and lightning fast with his guns. He drew first and asked questions later. But he was a drinker and a gambler, and was thought by many to be as bad as those he was supposed to control.

Many people were relieved when Bill Hickok was shot in the back while playing poker in Deadwood.

A posse shoots it out with outlaws. People power was an important part of law enforcement in the West. Shoot-outs usually ended with the outlaws giving themselves up or leaving town as one or two of them were killed by the posse.

THE EARPS

The Earp brothers are also remembered among the more infamous badge-holders of the Wild West. Virgil, a marshal of Tombstone, Arizona, pocketed local taxes. Wyatt, a saloon guard, was also a notorious gambler. Joined by brothers James and Morgan, the Earps tangled with a rival political gang, the Clanstons, at the OK Corral. The army had to be called in to restore order.

A U.S. deputy marshal's badge from 1895. Deputy marshals (right) often traveled in small groups with a wagon to use as a traveling jail.

Trees, telegraph poles, and even railroad bridges were used as gallows from which to hang a criminal.

37

STAGECOACHES

In the early days of the frontier, sending messages across the continent was very difficult. As the West opened up, it became vital to develop a swift transportation system from the east to the frontier, and back.

STAGECOACHES

Trade goods were carried in wagons or by mule train. Mail and passengers went on horseback or by stagecoach. The first stagecoach route opened in 1756 between Boston, Philadelphia, and New York.

TRAVEL IN THE WEST

Travel in the East was relatively simple but journeys to the West were more hazardous because of the greater distances, the lack of finished roads, and dangers from bad weather and attacks. In 1848, the journey from New York City to San Francisco could take four months by land.

OVERLAND MAIL COMPANY

The first attempt to connect the East to the West by an overland route came when John Butterfield, the founder of the American Express Company, set up the Overland Mail Company in 1857. His stagecoaches carried mail and passengers between St. Louis, Missouri, and San Francisco in California. Each coach was pulled by a team of four or six horses or mules. Hundreds of drivers, station attendants, and armed guards operated 139 stagecoach stations, and looked after hundreds of horses and mules.

John Butterfield's stagecoach route went through the states of Missouri, Arkansas, Texas, New Mexico, and Arizona.

Speed was everything in the Pony Express. Riders were all under 18 years old and chosen for their bravery. Often armed with just a Bowie knife, the riders relied on their speed to get them out of trouble (left). They rode only the best quality horses which were fed on a diet of corn to make them very fast. Only one Pony Express mail bag was lost in the history of the service, although many riders and station attendants were killed by Indians and bandits. The service was advertised by posters (below).

THE PONY EXPRESS

The first stagecoach journey from St. Louis to San Francisco took 23 days. In 1860, the freight company Russell, Majors & Waddell organized a direct Pony Express mail service from St. Joseph, Missouri, to Sacramento, California, in just ten days.

Each Pony Express rider could carry 20 pounds of mail locked in four leather boxes fitted into a special saddlebag called a mochila. The rider galloped between relay stations which were about 10–12 miles apart. At each station he mounted a fresh pony and transferred the mochila, often without stopping. Each rider rode about 75 miles in total, then passed the mochila to the next rider. In this way each delivery covered the 2,000-mile journey to the west coast in about 10 days. The Pony Express was glamorous, but the company lasted only 18 months. In October 1861, it went bankrupt when the Western Union company completed a transcontinental telegraph line.

An engraving of 1876, entitled The Progress of the Century, *features a telegraph machine and railroad which, as a form of communication and mail service, together brought about the end of the Pony Express.*

WELLS FARGO

In 1843, Henry Wells and James Fargo formed an express company to carry letters between Chicago and St. Louis. In 1866, Wells Fargo took over the Central Overland Mail & Express Company and its network of stagecoach routes, to become the only major stagecoach line. Soon there were Wells Fargo offices in every town and anything and everything was sent by their stagecoaches. But, gradually, stagecoach lines, too, went into decline, driven out of business by the new railroads.

THE IRON HORSE

Ordinary people traveled "Emigrant and Freight" in day cars, which were little better than cattle cars. They had hard wooden benches for seats and a central aisle. There was a stove at one end and a toilet at the other. Wealthy people traveled in luxurious cars, as shown in the see-through scene.

A Union Pacific poster of 1869 advertising the opening of the Atlantic to Pacific railroad. About this time, George Pullman and Ben Field introduced the "Pullman Palace Car." These sleeper cars soon became renowned for their comfort and elegance. Other specialty cars would quickly be designed.

In 1855, Henry Farnam built a railroad bridge across the Mississippi from Rock Island, Illinois, to Davenport, Iowa. It was a major step in transcontinental transportation. During the next 50 years, over 260,000 miles of track would be laid down—enough to circle the world 10 times.

THE CPR AND THE UPR

In 1862 Congress authorized the building of a transcontinental railroad by two companies. The Central Pacific Railroad (CPR) started in California and went east, and the Union Pacific Railroad (UPR) started in Nebraska and went west. Each company raced to build the most track.

CPR PROBLEMS

Central Pacific progress was slow going across the Sierra Nevada mountains. All the CPR's iron building supplies had to be made in the East and brought by ship to the west coast around Cape Horn. Then hundreds of workers deserted when gold and silver was discovered in Colorado and Nevada. In desperation the construction boss, Charles Crocker, looked to cheap, foreign laborers to supplement his track-laying crew. Thousands of Irish and Chinese workers were brought to the States to work on the railroads.

40

1 Wooden bridge
2 Rails and sleepers
3 Wood fuel
4 Driver
5 Firebox
6 Boiler tubes
7 Spark catcher
8 Whistle
9 Piston
10 Connecting rod

THE UPR

The Union Pacific had no mountains to cross, but it had other problems. West of the Mississippi, land surveyors had to brave Indian attacks, and cope with large herds of buffalo that often trampled route markers.

Most Union Pacific workers were Irish. They were nicknamed "Tarriers" (the Irish pronunciation of Terriers) because it was said they dug across the plains as enthusiastically as dogs digging for bones.

THE MEETING OF THE LINES

On May 10, 1869, the two railroad companies met at Promontory Point, Utah. Bands played as the final golden spike was driven into the last tie with a silver sledgehammer. Five days later regular rail service from Chicago to Sacramento went into operation. The long overland journey could now be done in eight days. Other railroad companies that were given government grants started building track and the railroad network rapidly expanded.

Trains were often delayed by landslides, floods, snow, and broken bridges, as shown in the see-through scene. Before hunters wiped out the buffalo, trains often had to wait several hours for a huge herd to cross the tracks.

41

INDUSTRIAL BOOM

By 1900, America had become the richest single country in the world. Dramatic changes could be seen everywhere. Industry boomed. Western cities grew at a fantastic rate. Old frontier towns became respectable and civilized.

POPULATION

Between 1860 and 1890 the population of the U.S. doubled to 63 million. About 10 million of the new people were immigrants from Europe. During the next 30 years, 15 million more immigrants arrived from all over the world. Some of them came to make a quick fortune and then return home, but most of them stayed on to become U.S. citizens. Many moved into northern cities where manufacturing jobs were plentiful. At the same time, people living in rural areas moved closer to cities, where better-paying jobs awaited.

The discovery of oil in Texas brought another boom to the state and created a new type of prospector, the wildcatter (lone driller). The oil industry became very important with the invention of the motor car. The Model T, the first car designed for ordinary people, was produced by Henry Ford in 1908. It transformed travel.

INDUSTRIAL GROWTH

After 1870, the increasing pace of settlement in the West created a massive new demand for industrial goods. Farmers wanted the latest agricultural equipment. The expanding railroad network needed steel rails, locomotives, and railroad cars. The need for railways, bridges, roads, canals, dams, and houses created a boom in the construction industry.

New factories and mines were created to meet this demand. The mineral wealth of the West was exploited by large mining corporations. Industries, which had mainly been small scale before the Civil War, now took on an important role.

> **In America, one could make pots of money in a short time, acquire immense holdings, wear a white collar and have polish on one's boots, and eat . . . meat on weekdays as well as on Sundays, even if one were but an ordinary workman.**
>
> — *Louis Adamic* —

Machines like the McCormick reaper mechanized farming on the prairies and made them into the breadbasket of America, and the largest wheat-producing area in the world.

A GOLDEN AGE

New industries boomed, producing every conceivable item from pig iron to ice. This new industrial age brought great wealth for some Americans. There were over 4,000 millionaires in the U.S. in 1900. Some, including Andrew Carnegie, Cornelius Vanderbilt, and John D. Rockefeller (who owned the giant Standard Oil Company), had fortunes of well over $100 million. Typical Americans lived more modest lives, but could still afford simple pleasures, such as viewing Barnum & Bailey's traveling circus or baseball, which was becoming the national sport.

NEW GOODS

Slowly but surely, more and more parts of the West began to look like the East. Suburbs grew and paved streets appeared. Stores displayed a tantalizing variety of consumer goods. Some product names soon became famous, such as Coca-Cola and Ivory Soap. In large cities, rich people shopped in new department stores. Ordinary people visited "five-and-dime" stores like Woolworth's to buy cheaper goods. Millions of Americans enjoyed a standard of living that was unknown anywhere else in the world. They could choose from a variety of fresh, canned, frozen, and processed foods. They ate meals in fast-food restaurants, and enjoyed hot dogs, hamburgers, and ice cream. They had central heating, electric light, and gas stoves. They traveled to work on electric cable cars.

THE DISAPPEARING FRONTIER

By 1900, most of the West had been settled. The Indians had either been killed or forced onto reservations. Much of the old wilderness had been plowed into fields or fenced into pasture land. The railroad, along with Samuel Morse's telegraph and the telephone, which had been invented by Alexander Graham Bell in 1876, brought communication to the farthest outposts of the West. The day of the gunfighter was over. Automobiles began to replace horses. Pioneering and the struggle to open the frontier had become history.

Settlers rush to stake their claims in the Oklahoma land rush, 1889. Former Indian lands were opened to settlers by the government and were taken by force. Within days, thousands of settlers arrived, buildings were erected, and shops and saloons were open for business. The last land rush was in 1911. After that, little unclaimed land remained in the West, and the frontier disappeared forever.

A Jewish market on Hester Street, New York, in the 1890s. Between 1870 and 1910, the population of the U.S. more than doubled, and by 1900 there were 3.5 million people living in New York. Many of them were immigrants.

Cities on the East Coast, like New York and Boston, were stopping-off points for many immigrants on their way west. A great number of them stayed in the cities and never made the journey inland.

43

END OF THE FRONTIER

The classic shoot-out between good and bad guy as portrayed in many cowboy films.

Although by **1900** the physical frontier and the pioneering way of life had disappeared, the independent spirit of the Wild West lived on. Many frontier ways have become part of the American lifestyle. Long after the frontier had disappeared, the legends remained.

CHANGING LEGENDS

However, the true stories of the Wild West have changed as they have been passed down until they have become almost unrecognizable. Distorted versions of "how the West was won" are evident in books, movies, and television.

From them have come popular Western legends such as the lone gunfighter who takes a stand against injustice no matter what the odds. These legends are so widely believed that it can be difficult to separate fact from fiction. Dime novels, for example, glorified outlaws such as Billy the Kid to the point that he is considered more a folk hero than a common criminal. Many Wild West legends originated in dime novels. These books,

In 1883, Buffalo Bill's "Wild West" show toured the U.S. and Europe for several years. It made the Wild West famous throughout the world.

so-called because they sold for about 10 cents, first appeared around 1855. Writers were paid 2 cents for every word. This encouraged them to write quickly, but meant that many of their tales were probably also exaggerated.

BUNTLINE AND BUFFALO BILL

Ned Buntline, who died in 1886, was one of the most famous dime novelists. He transformed Indian scout William F. Cody into Buffalo Bill, the romantic star of several of his 400 novels. One famous dime novel, *The Virginian* by Philadelphian Owen Wister, sold 50,000 copies in just two months. The book, dedicated to President Theodore Roosevelt, gave life to the strong, silent Western hero.

BUFFALO BILL'S SHOWS

In 1883, Buffalo Bill's famous Wild West shows began. Audiences in the East and Europe watched spectacular stagecoach holdups, Indian attacks, a re-enactment of Custer's last stand, roundups, rodeo riding, and shooting exhibitions by Annie Oakley. The shows were part circus and part pageant. They were show-business events designed to entertain rather than to depict Western events accurately. The shows gave birth to several western myths, including that of "savage" Indians who always attacked "innocent" settlers and were then driven off by great heroes.

THE SPIRIT OF THE WILD WEST

Although the frontier was tamed long ago, the pioneering spirit of the West lives on in the nation today. Pioneers were tough, independent, adaptable, and willing to face impossible odds to fulfill their dreams. And while history will always embrace the memory of larger-than-life figures such as Davy Crockett, Jesse James, and Buffalo Bill, it was the ordinary people—the men, women, and children—who set out for the frontier in hopes of building better lives for themselves, and built a nation in the process.

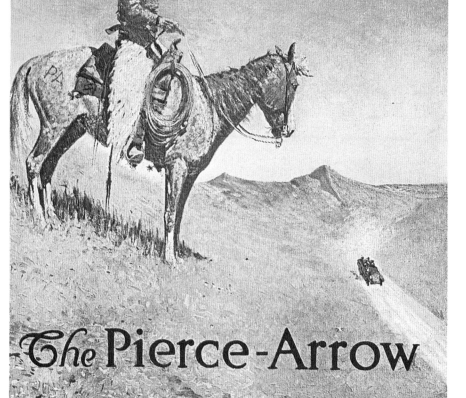

The Pierce-Arrow

The end of the Wild West—a Pierce-Arrow motor car advertisement of 1911 showing the wide open road and a cowboy.

A scene from The Undefeated, *made in 1969, starring Rock Hudson and John Wayne, and a poster for a 1922 cowboy silent movie. The first cowboy movie was made in 1903.*

45

KEY DATES AND GLOSSARY

Perhaps no period in history better illustrates the pursuit of the "American Dream" than the era of westward expansion. People from all walks of life and from countries around the world moved west in search of life, liberty, and happiness.

1783 United States of America is founded.

1787 U.S. Constitution written.

1800 Washington D.C. becomes the federal capital.

1803 Louisiana Purchase—over 828,000 square miles of land west of the Mississippi River—is bought from France.

1804 Meriwether Lewis and William Clark explore the Louisiana Territory.

1815 Congress authorizes construction of the Cumberland Road.

1818 The Convention of 1818 with Britain sets the U.S.-Canadian border at the 49th parallel from Minnesota to the Rocky Mountains.

1819 U.S. gains Florida from Spain.

1821 William Becknell blazes the Santa Fe Trail.

1825 Erie Canal opens, connecting the Great Lakes with the Hudson River.

1828 First railroad, the Baltimore and Ohio (B&O), breaks ground.

1836 Battle of the Alamo; Texas declares independence from Mexico.

1838 "Trail of Tears," a 1,200 mile journey forcing eastern Cherokee tribes to Oklahoma.

1846 Oregon Treaty divides Oregon east-west along the 49th parallel. U.S. and Mexico wage war.

1847 Mormons arrive in Utah.

1848 James Marshall discovers gold at Sutter's Mill, California. Mexican War ends.

1849 First gold prospectors arrive in California; Gold Rush begins.

1858 John Butterfield opens his overland stage route.

1860 Pony Express service starts.

1861 Civil War starts.

1862 Congress passes the Homestead Act.

1864 200 Cheyenne are massacred at Sand Creek by U.S. soldiers.

1865 Civil War ends. Abraham Lincoln is assassinated.

1866 The first bank robbery in the U.S. is committed by the James Gang.

1867 35,000 cattle travel the Chisholm Trail. U.S. buys Alaska from Russia.

1869 Transcontinental railroad completed.

1874 Joseph Gliddens patents barbed wire. Gold is discovered in the Black Hills.

1876 Battle of Little Bighorn.

1878 The Lincoln County range war between rival cattle ranchers begins.

1884 The world's first skyscraper built in Chicago.

Glossary

cannibalizing: the act of eating human flesh.

cholera: a disease caught by drinking impure water.

feud: quarrel between rival gangs or families.

guerillas: members of a covert, independent military force.

gunfighter: law officer who used a gun to uphold the law.

gunman/gunslinger: criminal who used a gun to break the law.

mochila: a saddle pouch.

pemmican: preserved food made by drying buffalo meat, pounding it into powder, and mixing it with hot fat.

plain: flat, mostly treeless, expanse of land.

range: open area of land over which animals can roam freely.

religious persecution: punishment of someone for their religious beliefs.

rustlers: cattle thieves.

staking a claim: the process by which a prospector or settler claimed a section of land by marking it with a stake or stakes on which were written the owner's name.

Quotations

George Ruxton was an English traveler. The mountain man he describes, Old Bill Williams, had been a Methodist preacher before he became a trapper. James Marshall was the man whose gold find started the California Gold Rush. Marshall's employer, John Sutter, made almost no money from the gold discovered on his land although a number of his employees became very rich. Octavius T. Howe was one of the thousands of people who traveled on wagon trains rolling westward. Joseph G. McCoy was a businessman who persuaded Texas ranchers to drive their cattle to the railhead at Abilene. Oliver M. Lee was a pioneering Texas rancher. Tom "Bear River" Smith was a marshal in the West who brought law and order to Abilene. Smith rarely carried a gun, generally preferring to subdue his man with a single punch. The memorial on his grave describes him as a "fearless hero." Louis Adamic was a Slovenian who emigrated to the U.S. in 1913, by which time the West was no longer wild.

The beauty and ruggedness of the landscape combined with the exciting action of the Wild West inspired many artists. One of the best known was Frederic Remington, who did nearly 3,000 paintings, drawings, and sculptures on western themes. He found subjects for his art while working as a cowboy. This painting by Remington is called Trailing Texas Cattle. *Collectors now pay millions of dollars for original Remingtons.*

INDEX

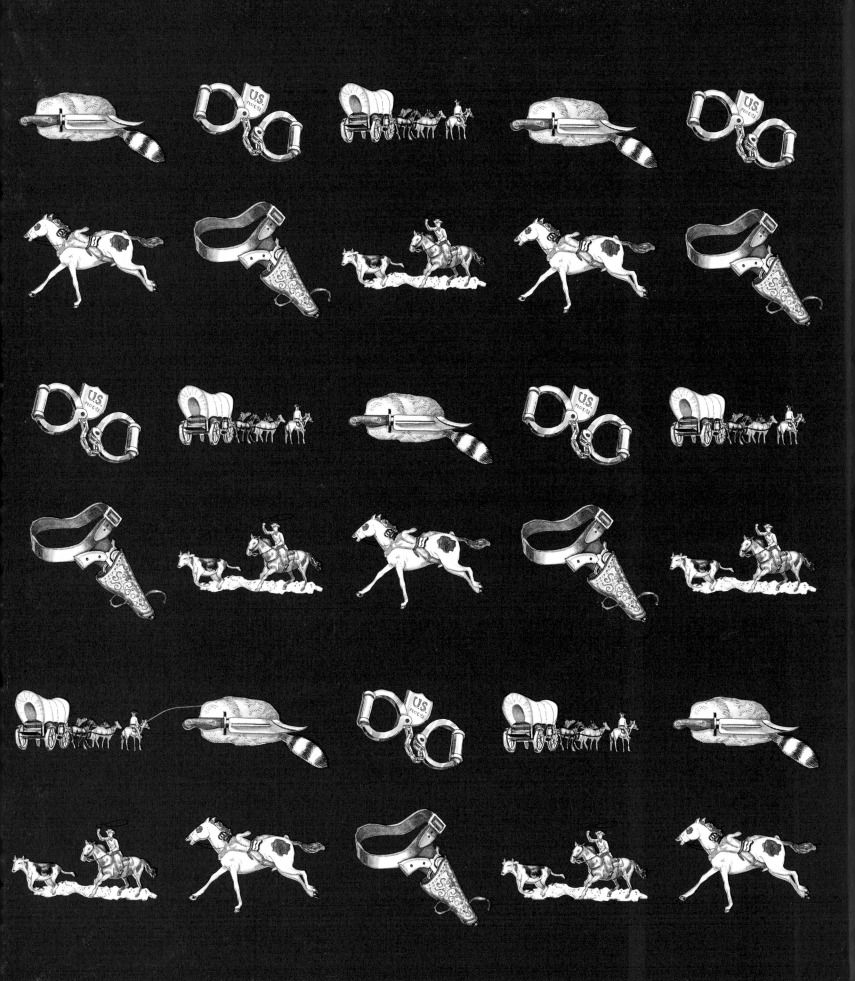